MONSTER HUNTERS
search for bigfoot

by Jan Fields
Illustrated by Scott Brundage

Calico

An Imprint of Magic Wagon
www.abdopublishing.com

www.abdopublishing.com

Published by Magic Wagon, a division of ABDO, PO Box 398166, Minneapolis, Minnesota 55439. Copyright © 2015 by Abdo Consulting Group, Inc. International copyrights reserved in all countries. No part of this book may be reproduced in any form without written permission from the publisher. Calico™ is a trademark and logo of Magic Wagon.

Printed in the United States of America, North Mankato, Minnesota.
032014
092014

**THIS BOOK CONTAINS
RECYCLED MATERIALS**

Written by Jan Fields
Illustrated by Scott Brundage
Edited by Tamara L. Britton
Cover and interior design by Candice Keimig

Library of Congress Cataloging-in-Publication Data

Fields, Jan, author.
  Search for Bigfoot / by Jan Fields ; illustrated by Scott Brundage.
     pages cm. -- (Monster hunters)
  Summary: After an encounter with a fake Bigfoot, the film crew of the
Internet series, Discover Cryptids, heads to the Florida swamps to search
for the "Skunk Ape"--but find a crooked ranger who hates Florida panthers,
instead.
  ISBN 978-1-62402-046-9
  1. Monsters--Juvenile fiction. 2. Curiosities and wonders--Juvenile fiction.
3. Video recording--Juvenile fiction. 4. Action photography--Juvenile fiction.
5. Adventure stories. 6. Florida--Juvenile fiction. [1. Monsters--Fiction.
2. Curiosities and wonders--Fiction. 3. Video recording--Fiction. 4. Adventure
and adventurers--Fiction.] I. Brundage, Scott, illustrator. II. Title.
  PZ7.F479177Sc 2015
  813.6--dc23
                                    2014005842

TABLE of CONTENTS

chapter 1

CHASED BY BIGFOOT

The pounding grew louder as the boys ran. Gabe Brown knew that didn't make sense. They should be getting farther away. Sometimes the sound boomed right behind them. Other times it seemed to be directly over their heads. Sometimes they left it behind for a while. After every few steps, a stone shifted under Gabe's feet or a root grabbed at his sneakers, keeping him from picking up speed in the thick forest.

The land ahead climbed steeply upward. Soon the boys were scrambling on all fours. Still, the pounding followed them, loud and insistent. Something smacked into Gabe's side, and he shrieked in surprise.

"Just me," Tyler gasped.

Gabe shot his best friend a look that he knew Tyler couldn't see. In the thick forest, the early evening might as well have been midnight.

They reached a pile of brush and fallen trees. The California woods were full of broken, half-rotted trees from the high winds of the last summer storm. They had to slow down to scramble through the gaps between the trees. The bellowing roar from behind kept them moving.

"We really made that thing mad," Tyler said as he climbed up onto the highest part of the tree fall.

"You think?" Sean said from behind them. Sean was the researcher for their team. Gabe recognized Sean's lecture tone as his friend added, "Most apes are territorial."

"So you're a Bigfoot believer now?" Tyler called back.

"My mind is always open."

"Don't let anything fall out."

Tyler had stopped to argue with Sean. It was his two friends' favorite pastime as far as Gabe could tell. He grabbed Tyler's arm and hauled him upward. "Fight later. Run now."

Keeping track of where they were in the dark was tough, but Gabe was almost certain that when they got over this ridge, they'd be overlooking the highway. Then all they had to do was follow the road. Eventually they'd either meet up with Ben or find people. Nice, safe people.

Gabe stretched to reach a branch on a fallen tree and hiked himself over the top. He dropped to the ground. At least, that was the plan. Instead, Gabe fell through the open air far longer than he expected. He finally hit the ground with a thud, knocking the wind out of him.

The ground sloped, and Gabe bounced downward. Brush and rocks battered him and he covered his face with his arms.

He finally managed the change in position and slid more slowly as he dug his sneakers into the slope. He reached out to the branches that slapped at him, trying to catch hold and stop.

The slope evened out and Gabe stumbled to his feet. He hurt everywhere, but he was proud of the fact that he could still stand. The light was better here, with no trees overhead. Gabe could see that he stood at the side of the highway.

He slowly spun in a circle as he heard the sound of tires crunching on the side of the road.

Bright lights shone in his eyes. He threw an arm up in front of his face.

"Gabe! Nice of you to drop in!"

Gabe recognized the voice of his stepbrother Ben and began a stumbling run toward his brother's van. "Bigfoot was chasing us!"

"Not exactly."

Gabe got close enough to see around the headlights. The side door was open and Ben held a handful of ragged fur. Gabe nearly shrieked again. Ben had caught Bigfoot!

Then he recognized what he was really seeing. A guy in an ape suit. "Aw, really?"

"Afraid so," Ben said. "And the thumps and bellows are recordings. The guy rigged up speakers all over in the woods."

Gabe slumped in disappointment.

Behind him, he heard the crash and shriek of Sean and Tyler, tumbling down the hill to join them.

chapter 2

THE ADVENTURE BEGINS

Gabe stretched his arm toward the backpack on the floor between his feet. The van rumbled over a bump. Gabe's seat belt pulled tight against the few lingering bruises from the Bigfoot chase, making him gasp. He twisted to reach a little farther. Finally he snagged a strap and hauled the backpack into his lap. He began rooting in the bag, hoping to find an overlooked snack.

"Why didn't you just unbuckle?" Sean asked from the seat beside him. Sean's eyes stayed on the tablet in his lap.

A deep voice boomed from thc driver's seat. "Because the van is moving!"

Ben worried a lot about safety. That was weird when you thought about it, since his job was hardly safe. Ben hunted monsters for a living. Well, some people said he hunted imaginary monsters. He was the creator and host of the Internet series *Discover Cryptids*. Cryptids are animals from legends that *might* really exist. So far, Ben had never seen a real cryptid, but he was always hopeful. So was Gabe, most of the time.

The search for Bigfoot had taken them from California to Florida. Sean poked one of the sore spots on Gabe's arm. "Fun fact!"

Gabe groaned and rubbed his arm. Sean collected weird facts like normal people collected coins. "Did you know that Clearwater, Florida, has the most lightning strikes per capita in the United States?"

Tyler pulled on his own seat belt to lean over their seat. "What is a capita?"

"Capita is a unit of population," Sean said.

"It means per person," Gabe explained. He

knew Tyler would soon get annoyed with Sean's love of big words to explain other big words.

"So everyone in Clearwater gets hit by lightning?" Tyler asked. "Why do they live there?"

"No," Sean said. "They have more lightning strikes relative to other cities."

Tyler snorted. "Now, I know you're making that up. How would the lightning know if they have relatives in other cities?"

Sean just groaned. "Forget it."

Tyler flopped back in his seat with his arms crossed. "You don't have to act like I'm stupid."

"I wasn't acting," Sean said.

"Hey, Ben," Gabe yelled up to his brother to distract his friends. "Do you think we could stop for something to eat? I need food."

Ben laughed. "Okay, we'll stop somewhere near Sarasota. I promise."

Gabe relaxed against the back of his seat. Sean, Gabe, and Tyler made up the "Monster

11

Hunters." For a long time, they'd just been back-up researchers for Ben's show. Ben and a team of grown-ups did the actual fieldwork and filmed the Internet show.

But suddenly Ben's whole team quit to go work for a cable TV network. The network offered to hire Ben too, but he turned them down. Ben believed his own show was more honest than the big TV shows. TV needed shows with lots of drama. *Discover Cryptids* stuck to the facts.

Ben was going to shut the show down, until Gabe and his friends volunteered. Gabe knew they could make the show together. Tyler was fantastic with technical stuff. Sean remembered everything he ever read—and he read a lot. And Gabe kept his two friends on track—*most of the time.*

Ben was currently on a Bigfoot kick. Sean had done some research and learned that this cryptid was known by many names. It was called the Fouke Monster in Arkansas and Bigfoot in California. In the Pacific Northwest, it was known as Sasquatch. In Florida, the creature was called the Skunk Ape. Sean said native peoples in Asia's Himalayas called a similar cryptid Yeti.

Gabe's attention was brought back into the van when they finally pulled into a little roadside restaurant. Gabe's stomach growled louder than his mom's crabby Chihuahua.

"I could eat an alligator," Tyler moaned.

Ben pointed at the menu printed above the service window. "You'll have to settle for catfish. But it looks like the tables are near the water. If an alligator creeps up on us, you can eat it."

"I might try."

When they finally got their food, Gabe bit into his catfish. The crunch of the crisp batter and juicy fish made his stomach growl again.

Tyler laughed. "I keep hearing growls. Maybe Bigfoot is lurking around here."

A man from a nearby booth scowled in their direction. "Now, we call it Skunk Ape around here, and it's nothing to make jokes about."

"Have you seen it?" Ben asked.

"I have," the man said. "Once. When I was driving back from a camping trip down in Big Cypress."

"Could you tell us what you saw?" Ben asked.

The man leaned closer to them and said, "At first, I thought it was a man in a thick coat walking funny. But no one would wear a coat like that in the swamp heat. A man would drown in his own sweat that way. I was looking right at a Skunk Ape."

"Did it stink?" Tyler asked.

The man shook his head. "I didn't get that close. I suggest you don't get too close either. That ape could tear your head clean off."

Gabe shifted nervously in his seat and rubbed his neck. It was the one part of his body with no bruises from their last adventure. He hoped it stayed that way.

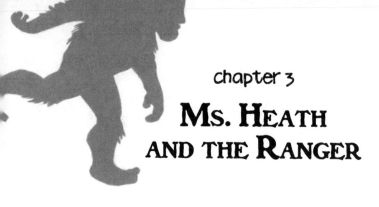

chapter 3

Ms. Heath
and the Ranger

With the slow-moving canal in the background, Ben interviewed the man as he talked about the Skunk Ape. Gabe held the camera. He could tell his brother was secretly excited. They'd barely started and they already had an interview with a witness.

Back in the car Gabe stared out the window and wondered what they would see in the Florida swamps. Tyler tapped on the window from behind him. "Are those coconut trees?"

Sean glanced up from his tablet and shook his head. "Cabbage palms. It's the Florida state tree."

Finally they pulled in at the campground that bordered Big Cypress National Preserve. Ben had rented one of the small cabins for their base camp. From there, they could investigate deeper in the swamp.

"Hey," Tyler yelled, pointing. "Look, they have a gorilla photo op."

Gabe turned and spotted the big wooden cutout mounted on the back of a trailer. It pictured a gorilla clutching a squirming tourist. A circle had been cut in the picture. You could put your head through and pretend to be the tourist to get a picture taken.

Gabe took a step closer. "I think that's supposed to be a Skunk Ape."

Sean folded his arms over his chest. "That is clearly a gorilla. And gorillas do not attack people like that."

"Maybe really cranky gorillas do," Tyler said.

Ben shushed them as a tall, deeply tanned woman walked toward them. She wore a sleeveless shirt, jeans, and a cowboy hat. "Ah, Ms. Heath, I assume," Ben called out. "It was nice of you to drive up and meet us. I'm sorry we're a little late."

"No problem. It gave me a chance to set up my Skunk Ape." She pointed toward the wooden sign. "Tourists love it, but the park folks will be along soon to tell me I have to move it. They have no sense of humor." She rolled her eyes, then thrust her hand out toward Ben. "You must be Ben Green. I watched all the episodes of *Discover Cryptids* after you called. Nice show." She looked around as Ben shook her hand. "Where's your crew?"

"Right here," Ben said. "This is my brother Gabe. He'll be handling the camera. Tyler handles the rest of the gear, and Sean is our head researcher. Guys, this is Tanya Heath. She collects information about the Skunk Ape."

The tall woman blinked. Then she shook hands with each of the boys. "You better watch out," she said. "The Skunk Ape isn't the only thing in the swamp that can run off with a kid. We've got alligators, panthers, bears, and pythons."

"Some of the reports sound like they could have been bears," Ben said.

Ms. Heath shook her head and frowned. "Our bears aren't that big. You're not trying to prove the Skunk Ape is a trick, are you?"

Ben shrugged. "It helps in the investigation to rule out possible other answers."

Ms. Heath pushed the cowboy hat back on her head. "I don't think anyone is likely to confuse one of our little old bears with the Skunk Ape."

Sean added, "Of course, in the dark, a man in a fur coat could look a lot like an ape."

Ms. Heath turned and squinted at Sean. "You feel this heat? Who would wander around this swamp in a coat? I know what I saw. And it wasn't a man in a coat. It was a creature."

Ben cleared his throat. "We like to consider all possibilities during an investigation."

The woman snorted. "Well, you go on out in the swamp looking for men in coats. But don't expect my help."

Suddenly they all heard someone shouting. "Hey! Get that thing out of this campground!"

Ms. Heath turned around and winked at the boys, all signs of her anger gone. "See? No sense of humor."

The man storming toward them wore a park uniform consisting of dark green pants and a short-sleeved gray shirt. Above all of it, he had a fierce scowl. "I've warned you about that thing before, Tanya. This is not a cheap tourist trap."

"Just having a little fun, Carl," she said, grinning. "Thought I'd wake things up around here and give your campers some fun."

"Things are lively enough." The man turned to look at Ben. "Are you with her?"

"Not exactly," Ben replied. "Though I do hope for her help. I'm Ben Green. I talked to someone here about filming my show?"

"Oh." The man's face darkened still more and he took a deep drink from a water bottle before speaking. "The monster hunter. If it were up to

me, we'd pass on that rubbish. But it wasn't my call. Just be sure you don't interfere with the other campers or with the wildlife or make any messes you don't clean up."

"We'll do our best, Ranger…?" Ben said.

"Carl Rain," the man said.

"Good to meet you." Ben looked around the campground. "Could you point us toward our cabin? We have gear to unload before dark."

Ms. Heath laughed. "Dark is when things get lively around here."

"Only if you're interested in alligator calls and mosquitoes," Ranger Carl said. He took another gulp of water.

"I know the way," Ms. Heath said. "I'll show you. We can talk about the best Skunk Ape spotting areas around here."

The ranger snorted, spun on his heel, and headed back the way he'd come.

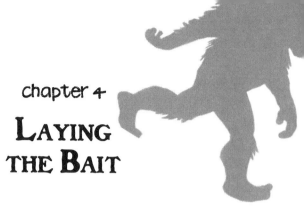

chapter 4
LAYING THE BAIT

Their cabin was the farthest from the main road. Ben wanted to be well away from the other campers. All the research online said Bigfoot creatures were shy and didn't like loud noises.

As the guys carried equipment into the cabin, Ms. Heath bellowed Skunk Ape stories. Gabe figured the Skunk Ape must be hiding far, far away. He was about ready to head for the swamps himself. When the last bit was hauled into the cabin, Ms. Heath announced she was leaving.

"Do you want me to drive you back to your truck?" Ben asked.

"No. I like walking this time of evening.

You never know what you'll see. You give me a call when you're ready to go out for a Skunk Ape hunt."

"Thanks," Ben said.

After she'd gone, Gabe walked over to his brother. "Are you really going to call her?" he asked. "She's kind of loud."

Ben laughed. "No, we'll do our actual fieldwork quietly. Later, we'll get her to tell a story or two for the camera."

Tyler and Sean walked over to join them near the van. "It's not as smelly here as I expected," Tyler said.

"Swamps can produce methane and other gases," Ben said. "Usually you only have a smell when there's gas."

"Kind of like Gabe," Tyler said, laughing hard at his own joke.

"Swamps are very important to the state," Sean said, launching into "fun fact" mode. "The thick vegetation filters the water. Swamps slow down the flow of water during heavy rains. That helps stop flooding. And the swamp is a major habitat for wildlife and plant life."

"Wildlife like stinky Skunk Apes," Tyler said.

"We hope," Ben agreed.

"Swamp gas is sometimes blamed for the strong smells associated with Skunk Apes," Sean added. "Some people believe that Skunk Apes sleep in alligator dens where methane gas collects."

"Are we going to do any filming tonight?" Gabe asked.

"Not exactly," his brother said. "I want to set up a motion camera and some bait. We'll see if we pick up any images while we sleep."

"That's the kind of work I like," Tyler said. "The kind where nothing is chasing us."

They quickly finished piling everything in the cabin and claiming beds. Then Ben gathered the things they would need to lay the bait. "Okay," he called. "Let's go."

"If you don't need me, I'm going to stay here," Sean answered. He sat cross-legged on the sofa bed, his eyes glued to his tablet. "Someone uploaded a new Skunk Ape video online. I want to check it out."

"Okay. Be sure to save the link. I'll look at it when we get back." Ben hustled them out the door. They headed down a narrow trail and into the denser undergrowth. The light was fading. Eerie shadows stretched deep into the woods.

Finally Ben stopped next to a stunted palmetto tree and opened the cooler he was carrying. "Oh gross!" Tyler yelped, fanning the air. "That smells rank."

"It is a little rank," Ben admitted. He pulled out a whole chicken and then dumped some overripe fruit on top of it. "There's some debate about what Skunk Apes eat, but we know smell

signals food." He pointed to one of the pale, skinny trees on the other side of the path. A half-rotted log lay next to the tree. "Gabe, can you attach this night vision camera to that tree? Make sure it's looking down on this bait."

Using the log as a step stool, he wired the camera to the tree as high up as he could reach. Gabe clung to the tree and twisted halfway around it to see the view screen. It was pointed right at the bait. "Got it!"

"Good. Don't forget to wrap the case in the plastic grocery bag," Ben said as he used a stick to spread out the bait a little. "The weather can be unpredictable here. That camera is water resistant, but it's also expensive."

"All set," Gabe called before he hopped off the log.

"Now can we eat?" Tyler asked.

"You can think about food after handling that stuff?" Gabe asked.

Tyler shrugged and headed up the trail. "I can think about food anytime."

Gabe cast one last glance at the disgusting mess on the ground. "As long as we aren't having chicken."

Ben laughed and fell in line behind Gabe. "Nope, the chicken is all for our ape friend."

As they entered the cabin, Gabe still felt like the stink of the chicken and fruit was stuck in his nose. "I don't know how any animal could think that smells yummy."

"Yeah, ripe chicken and even riper fruit, yuck." Tyler waved a hand in front of his face as if he could still smell the bait too.

"So we might just end up with raccoon pictures," Tyler said.

"I imagine a number of animals would find that combination tasty," Sean said, looking up from his tablet. "The Everglades are home to raccoons, opossums, foxes, black bears, panthers, and alligators. Any of those would be drawn to one or all of those things."

"Probably," Ben admitted as he headed over to the small kitchen area and began unpacking their food supplies. "I'm not expecting to film a Skunk Ape on the first try, but you never know."

Tyler and Gabe piled onto the sofa bed to look at the Skunk Ape film Sean had found. It wasn't very clear, and Gabe thought it could easily be a guy in a coat. "The problem with this video,"

Sean said, "is that there is no way to determine scale. The growth around the image doesn't really hint at it being a giant ape."

Tyler snorted. "The problem to me is that it's so blurry. How come no one with a decent camera ever sees a Bigfoot?"

"They're surprise sightings," Ben said as he dumped beans into a pot on the stove. "And mostly at night. Cell phones don't film well in the dark or at long distances."

Gabe got up from the sofa and walked to the nearest window. It was completely dark outside.

Just then a howling shriek came from outside. The tiny hairs on the back of Gabe's neck stood up. Ben dropped the pot of beans onto the small cabin table and sprinted for the door. The boys followed him outside.

They peered into the total darkness. Anything could be peering back at them—including a Skunk Ape.

"Do you think that was the ape?" Tyler whispered.

"It might have been a Florida panther," Sean said. "They don't roar, but they do make a kind of screechy growl. I could probably find a sound file online that we could listen to."

"A panther?" Tyler squeaked as he edged back into the cabin. "Great. A huge, meat-eating cat is way less scary than a Skunk Ape."

"Whatever it is," Ben told them as he began herding Gabe and Sean inside, "Let's hope it took our bait so we can see its smiling face in the morning."

"Yeah," Gabe agreed. As long as they didn't see it before then.

chapter 5

CALL OF THE SKUNK APE

Gabe woke to a snarling shriek. He jumped off the top bunk and landed on Tyler, who had jumped out of the bottom bunk.

"Ouch, get off!"

"What was that?" Gabe demanded. His eyes darted around the cabin, and he spotted Sean sitting on the couch. His laptop was open in his lap.

"That was the Florida panther," Sean announced happily. "I knew I could find a sound file. That sounded very much like what we heard last night."

"Why didn't you warn us before you did that?" Tyler said.

Sean raised an eyebrow. "You were sleeping.

I didn't want to bother you."

"You didn't want to bother me?" Tyler yelled.

"I'm nice that way."

"Enough with the yelling," Ben said as he walked out of the cabin's tiny bathroom. "And no more animal sound files unless you turn down your speakers."

Sean shrugged. "I thought it would sound more realistic with the volume up."

"There's such a thing as too much realism," Ben said as he walked over to the couch. "Do you have the feed from the camera at the bait site?"

Sean nodded and grinned. "I was just waiting for everyone to wake up."

"That had to be the world's worst alarm clock," Gabe said.

Sean cued up the camera, but nothing happened for several long minutes. The pile of bait blended in with the rest of the ground in the night vision camera.

Suddenly the feed blanked out as something covered the lens. Then the camera again began recording the swamp brush. The picture jumped and swung until Gabe felt a little queasy. Clearly something was pulling the camera out of the tree. After that, the scene was a blur. The camera was moving too fast to focus on anything. When the

image switched to the rocky ground, the video simply stopped.

Before Sean even closed his laptop, Ben was heading for the door. The three boys followed him. When they reached the rough trail, Gabe wished he'd changed out of his pajamas or at least put on his sneakers. Some of the grass was seriously prickly.

A couple of chicken bones marked the spot where the bait had been. The camera was squashed, and the insides were partly on the outside. It definitely wouldn't be taking pictures anytime soon.

"How much force would it take to squash a camera like that?" Gabe asked.

Ben gently picked up the camera and turned it over and over in his hands. "More than I could come up with."

"Unless you bashed it with a rock," Sean said. "I believe that would work."

Ben shrugged. "I don't know why it would." He raised his eyes to his brother. "Tonight we camp out and see what's out here."

Gabe swallowed hard. He wondered if they'd make it out of this adventure with nothing but bruises.

They walked back to the cabin in silence. Gabe kept sneaking glances into the swamp. He noticed Tyler and Sean doing the same. Ben's attention was focused on the smashed camera in his hands.

Near the cabin they heard a hearty yell. Tanya Heath stomped up to them. She grinned at the three boys in pajamas. "Y'all like to get an early start, I see."

Gabe crossed his arms to cover up the faded Superman symbol on his pajama shirt.

"We set out a bait trap last night," Ben said as he held up the smashed camera. "But apparently the camera was more appealing."

The woman nodded. "The Skunk Ape."

"Maybe," Ben said. "Though we may have heard a panther last night."

She shrugged. "The call of the Skunk Ape can sound a lot like a panther. I can tell the difference, of course."

"Do panthers come this close to campgrounds?" Sean asked.

"Panthers go wherever they like. They're dangerous animals." The group looked up to see Ranger Carl coming through the brush, carrying his water bottle. When he reached them, he glared at Ms. Heath. "You brought that Skunk Ape cutout back."

"Did I?" she asked. "I must have forgotten it was in my wagon."

Gabe couldn't imagine how you could drive around without noticing a giant gorilla sign on your truck trailer.

"Have you seen panthers around here?" Ben asked Ranger Carl.

The ranger nodded and took a sip from his water bottle. "A male was hit by a car on the highway a few weeks ago. I've been seeing a female lurking near some of the roads around here. You need to be careful with food."

"It wasn't a cat that mangled that camera," Ms. Heath insisted. "That was a Skunk Ape, plain and simple."

Ranger Carl stepped closer and looked at the camera. "Or someone bashed it with a rock."

"Do you get much vandalism?" Ben asked.

The ranger shook his head "We're a little far out for that. We get littering though."

Ben nodded, his forehead creased with thought.

Ms. Heath glared at the ranger, then said, "Let me help with your investigation. I can help you avoid problems like this."

Ben nodded. "I appreciate the offer. As long as you're here, I should get some footage of you yelling about your encounters."

"Yelling?" she asked, narrowing her eyes.

"Oh, I meant telling." Ben's smile was completely innocent, but the boys had trouble fighting down laughter.

The ranger rolled his eyes. "I've heard all those stories more than I care to, and I've got plenty of productive things to do. Let me know if you need anything."

Ben nodded. "Thanks." He rubbed his hands together. "Okay, guys, let's get the equipment and film this clip."

Gabe glanced down at his dirty socks. "Can we get dressed first?"

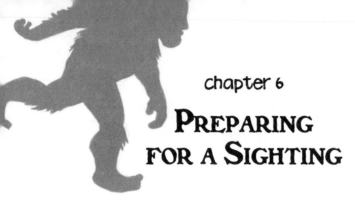

chapter 6

PREPARING FOR A SIGHTING

Tanya Heath clearly loved being on camera. She stomped around to imitate a Skunk Ape and even bellowed out her version of a Skunk Ape call.

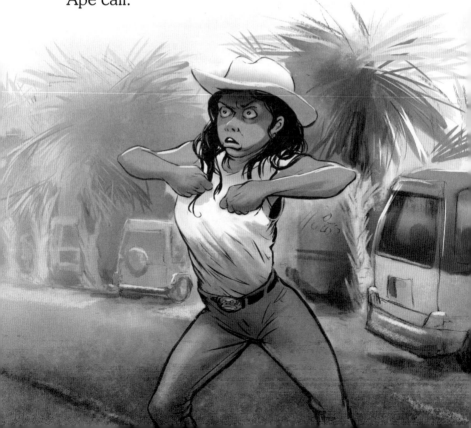

"That isn't what we heard," Sean said after she shrieked loudly. "So we probably heard a panther."

The woman shrugged. "Maybe. Those panthers are nothing but nuisances. Did you know the conservation nuts actually brought in Texas cougars to help build up the breed? That doesn't make sense. It's gotten so bad the orange growers are scared to walk around in their own groves because of those critters."

"I've been doing some reading," Sean said. "Panthers used to roam all over the Southeast. Now there are just over 100 Florida panthers left in the wild. The cats need a lot of room to roam without clashing with one another. Development and the gradual move south of the orange groves aren't leaving much room for panthers."

For once Tyler caught what Sean was saying. "You mean orange growers aren't finding

41

panthers in their groves. The cats are finding oranges in their territory."

"Oranges are a lot more useful to Florida than killer cats," Ms. Heath said. "You children don't understand the realities of life down here."

Ben crossed his arms. "Well, I don't suppose I understand it either."

She narrowed her eyes at Ben. "I thought you were down here looking for Skunk Apes. You let me know if you get back to that." Then she turned sharply and stormed off.

"Oops, I guess we don't get any more help from the Skunk Ape expert," Gabe said.

Ben turned and headed into the cabin. "Anyone as attention seeking as Tanya Heath is sure to be back. For now, let's get ready for tonight's trip into the swamp."

Ben supervised the collecting of supplies. Sean's contribution was to sit on the couch and stare at the laptop.

"What are you doing?" Gabe asked suspiciously.

"Yesterday I began cataloging similarities between Skunk Ape sightings," Sean said. "I wanted to finish doing that, as it should suggest the best place to search for them."

Ben walked over to the couch. "I thought this swamp was a major source of the sightings."

"It is," Sean said slowly. "But mostly from the roads around here. In fact, the vast majority of Skunk Ape sightings have come from people driving these roads in the dark."

"Why would Skunk Apes hang out next to the road?" Gabe asked. "I thought they were shy."

"It does seem odd," Sean agreed.

"Maybe that's just because there are so many more people on the roads than in the swamp itself," Ben suggested.

Sean nodded slowly, again deep in thought. "Possibly, but there were about 20 million visitors

43

to Florida's state parks in 2010. Park land seems like a natural place for Skunk Apes to hide, but the sightings come much more from roads than parks."

"Then maybe we should put off the swamp camping for one more night and do a little night driving," Ben said. "At worst, we'll catch some wildlife on film. Viewers like that too."

"We may get so much footage from tonight that we won't need to camp out with the bugs and snakes," Sean said.

"Unless we find a Skunk Ape hitchhiker who wants to give an interview," Ben said, "we're still going to camp. If we get mostly ready today, it'll save time tomorrow." He turned to Gabe. "Bring in the sleeping bags from the van. I want to check out the area around the bait again and snap photos if I find any tracks."

A few minutes later, Gabe waddled to the cabin door with his arms full. He tried to free three fingers to turn the knob. It didn't open. He kicked the door and waited for someone to open it. Finally he shifted the load. One of the sleeping bags fell on the ground. He opened the door and gathered up everything he dropped.

When he staggered in, he found Sean still on the couch. "Hey, didn't you hear me knock?"

"It sounded like kicking," Sean said.

"And you didn't think to open the door?"

"I'm very busy. If I'm going to be forced to spend the night with nature, I must be prepared," Sean said.

"This site recommends freezing water in jugs to help keep food cold while also offering plenty of drinking water," Sean said.

"I'm ahead of you there," Ben said. "I put the jugs in the freezer here yesterday." He walked over and hauled a jug out of the freezer and shook it. It still sloshed slightly. "They should be solid by the time we need them."

Gabe was impressed that Ben never seemed to get tired of Sean's "suggestions." Gabe was certainly getting tired of them. He kicked the couch as he came in from the van with the tarps in his arms. "You could help."

"I am helping."

"Help with the carrying."

"My brain is stronger than my arms," Sean said. "I'm going with my strengths. I found a site that suggests you never sit on any of the fallen trees and stumps in the swamp. Apparently you can get something called 'red bugs' and end up in the hospital."

Gabe froze, trying to remember if he'd sat on the fallen log near the bait site. He remembered climbing on it, but not sitting on it. "Can you get the red bugs from standing on fallen trees?"

Sean shrugged. "It doesn't say."

Gabe hurried to the bathroom for a shower, while Ben and Tyler checked out all of the camera equipment. Gabe scrubbed until his skin was red and he stopped feeling like bugs were crawling on him.

He found Ben carefully packing cameras. "Did you find any tracks at the bait site?" he asked.

Ben shook his head. "Just shoe prints. I assumed they were ours, unless the Skunk Ape has taken to wearing shoes."

"He might have," Sean called from the couch, "if it's a man in a suit."

Gabe thought of the man in the Bigfoot suit they'd caught in California. Surely not all cryptids were fake.

"I think Gabe and I should ask other campers if they've seen any Skunk Apes," Tyler suggested.

"That's not a bad idea," Ben said. "Don't bug anyone."

"No problem!" Gabe and Tyler raced out of the cabin, happy to escape.

chapter 7

BRIEF ENCOUNTER

The air outside felt thick. Gabe's T-shirt was damp by the time they reached the main camping area. "I hope we find someone who heard that weird screaming last night," he said.

Unfortunately, they didn't. No one had heard anything. No one had seen the Skunk Ape. One group of teenagers even laughed at them. Gabe turned to walk away when one of the guys yelled, "Wait, don't go away mad. Actually Zack saw something."

Gabe turned around, waiting for the punch line. "Yeah?"

"He saw someone skulking around the campsite in a coat," the guy said.

"Oh? Is Zack around?"

The guy shook his head. "No, his girlfriend didn't like all the mosquitoes. They drove up to the theme parks."

"But he saw a guy in a coat?" Gabe asked.

The guy shrugged. "He said he did. But who would wear a fur coat here? You'd die of heat."

"That's true," Tyler agreed as he wiped sweat from his face with his shirt.

"Was he sure it wasn't a bear?" Gabe asked.

"Only if it was smarter than the average bear." The teenager laughed. "He said it had a flashlight."

Asking questions kept them busy until suppertime. After sweating the whole time, Gabe wished they'd brought a water bottle. No wonder the ranger carried one all the time. Finally, he and Tyler staggered through the cabin door, gasping. "Water!"

Ben rolled his eyes at their dramatics. "When I was in college, I worked at a theme park. I wore this huge head and furry outfit. I probably lost a couple pounds every day just from sweating. You do that, and you really find out what it means to be thirsty."

"It doesn't make sense," Gabe said as he gulped water. "High humidity means there's water in the air, right?"

Ben nodded.

"So I ought to be less thirsty. It feels like I'm breathing water."

Sean looked up from his computer. "Heat makes you sweat. As the sweat evaporates, you feel cooler. In high humidity, your sweat won't evaporate. The air is already full of water. You never feel cooler, so you sweat away more and more of your water. That's why you feel so thirsty."

"Just remember to carry water from now on," Ben said. "Let's grab some supper and go look for Skunk Apes."

Over supper, Gabe and Tyler told them about

the teenager who saw a man in a coat. Ben raised an eyebrow. "If there is someone pretending to be a Skunk Ape, I can't imagine why."

"Well, the guy we caught in California in the Bigfoot suit was trying to scare people away so he could cut trees illegally," Gabe said. "Could it have been something like that?"

Sean shook his head. "Wetlands don't produce that kind of timber."

"Well, those guys might have been putting us on," Tyler said. "They seemed like jokers."

After supper, they drove along the mostly empty roads around the swamp. The sky turned gold and orange as the sun set. Ben drove slowly, and the others stared out the windows. Gabe called out when he spotted glowing eyes near the side of the road. It was a deer.

"Do people's eyes glow like that?" Gabe asked.

"No," Sean volunteered from the seat behind him. "Nocturnal animals have special light reflecting cells in their eyes. It helps them see in the dark. Humans don't. Neither do most primates."

"But I've seen photos of Skunk Apes with glowing red eyes," Tyler insisted.

Ben leaned over the wheel to watch the road carefully. "Skunk Apes may have the reflecting cells, since they're nocturnal. Or you may be seeing the usual red-eye from flash photos."

"So if we see eyes glowing alongside the road, it's not the Skunk Ape," Tyler said. "Unless it is. We don't get a lot of sure things in this job."

Ben laughed. "No, you certainly don't." Then he slowed the van even more. "Look, an armadillo!"

A small animal hurried across the road, looking like a tank with legs.

"Some of those small animals or glowing eyes might make good footage," Ben said. "Grab a camera, Gabe. And watch for photo ops."

Tyler passed Gabe a camera.

Ben increased speed until they were no longer creeping along the narrow paved road. Suddenly something raced out in front of the van. Ben slammed on the brakes and turned

the wheel hard, throwing everyone against their seat belts. The van rumbled off the highway and into a low ditch.

"Is everyone okay?" Ben asked.

The boys groaned. "Yeah."

"What *was* that?" Tyler asked. "It was big."

"Panther," Ben said. He shifted the van into reverse and tried to pull out of the ditch. The wheels spun. "You guys get out. Maybe I can do this when the van is lighter."

"Out there?" Tyler yelped. "With the panther?"

"The panther will be long gone," Ben said. "It was running. Plus, it wouldn't hang around after almost being hit."

"Just get out," Sean said, dragging Tyler along with him as he opened the van door and climbed out. Gabe walked up to the road to wait for Ben to pull out of the ditch. He turned on the camera and began scanning the brush beside the road.

A mosquito whined near his ear and he

swatted at it, making the camera jump. He spotted a tall outline off in the brush.

He lowered the camera and walked slowly across the road for a better look. When the hulking figure moved, he caught sight of it.

He kept the camera pointed at the moving creature. Was it the Skunk Ape?

Suddenly the huge creature turned toward Gabe. Gabe backed up fast, scrambling up the slight incline. When he hit the pavement, he tripped. The camera swung upward and Gabe caught sight of a furry arm swinging at him as he tumbled backward onto the road.

The roar of the van digging itself out of the ditch distracted Gabe. He turned toward the sound. When he looked back, the creature was gone. "Hey, guys!" he yelled. "I saw something. Something big."

"Was it the panther?" Tyler asked.

"No. It might have been a person," Gabe

said as Tyler hauled him to his feet. "It was big enough. Or it might have been a bear on its back legs. Anyway, it was big. I think I made it mad."

"Come on, guys," Ben yelled from the van. "What are you doing?"

"Gabe saw the Skunk Ape!" Tyler yelled.

"That would be very unlikely," Sean answered as he walked closer to them. "The van has been making a lot of noise. Skunk Apes are shy."

"This one wasn't," Gabe told him. "It came after me. I caught it on camera."

As they walked toward the van, a line of cars suddenly zoomed past them on the road. "Where did all these cars come from?" Gabe asked.

"That's an interesting question," Ben said. "This road was practically deserted before. Hop in and let's see what we can find."

They drove down the road for nearly two miles, passing cars coming toward them several times. Finally they reached a high school, where a parking lot was emptying out. A big sign announced a fund-raising event.

"Well, we know where the cars came from," Ben said. "I'm going to pull in here so we can take a look at those photos."

Gabe called up the photos on the camera's small view screen. Even with such small photos, it was clear he'd caught sight of *something* moving through the brush, though the camera swung wildly when the creature moved toward Gabe.

"We need to look at these on the laptop," Sean said.

Ben took the camera from his brother and went through the photos again. "It certainly looks like something two-legged."

"It was," Gabe said. "It came after me. I know that for sure."

chapter 8

PHYSICAL PROOF

When they pulled up in front of the cabin, the boys practically raced for the door. As usual, Sean beat them to the laptop and transferred pictures from the camera to the computer.

"You didn't hold the camera still," Sean scolded as he clicked through the blurry photos.

"That thing was coming after me!"

"If it was coming after me," Tyler added, "I wouldn't have taken pictures. I would have climbed on top of the van and screamed."

"There are no accounts of a Bigfoot creature hurting anyone," Sean said. "Well, not since 1829 when a Skunk Ape in Georgia pulled the heads off five hunters."

"What?" Gabe yelped.

"Some people believe that was just a legend," Sean said. "And the hunters did shoot the Skunk Ape first. It was probably mad about that."

"You're not making me feel all that much better. That thing I saw seemed really mad."

Ben walked into the cabin as they were talking. "Well, I looked over the van. The trip into the ditch didn't cause any damage. So, how do the photos look?"

"Blurry," Sean said.

Ben frowned and peered at a photo that mostly showed brush with only a small bit of something fuzzy in the lower corner. "What were you doing here?"

"Falling down," Gabe said. "The thing saw me and ran at me. I guess I panicked."

Ben ran through the video. "You clearly saw *something*. I wonder if we could clear any of these up." He paused at one of the clearest photos. "You know, that looks like a guy in a costume."

"Who would wander around the swamp in a Skunk Ape costume?" Tyler asked.

"Someone wanting to get on our show?" Gabe guessed.

"But how would the person know we were going to be driving around and taking photos?" Ben asked. "Did either of you boys tell anyone?"

Gabe and Tyler shook their heads.

"We weren't really seeing a lot of traffic until that school event let out," Sean said.

"Maybe it was those cars the 'Skunk Ape' was waiting for," Ben suggested. "After all, anyone local would know about that event. And we know one person who is very interested in keeping the Skunk Ape stories going."

The boys shouted, "Tanya Heath."

"Sean, do you think you can clear up any of these photos?" Ben asked. "Even a little would help."

"I'll try," Sean agreed. He stared at the screen

silently for a moment. "Do you think the panther was running from the person in the suit?"

"It's hard to say," Ben said. "If so, the person probably never saw the cat until it bolted."

Sean nodded, but his face was still clouded with thought. "I might research panthers too."

"You do that, but don't forget about the photos. Our next step is to spend the night in the swamp," Ben said.

Gabe was sure he wouldn't sleep a wink after nearly getting his head knocked off by a Skunk Ape. Instead, he slept like a log. He woke to his brother shaking him.

"Hop up," Ben said. "I want to go chat with Ranger Carl. Want to come?"

"Yeah, sure." Gabe quickly changed into shorts and a T-shirt. Sean was sitting at the small table in the cabin, working on clearing up the Skunk Ape footage. Tyler sat beside him, offering suggestions between huge spoonfuls of cereal.

"You coming, Tyler?" Gabe asked.

His friend shook his head. "Too hot."

"It *is* Florida," Gabe said.

Gabe and Ben found the ranger near the station house. Gabe noticed dark circles under the man's eyes. "You look tired," he said.

"Too hot to sleep," Ranger Carl said. "Can I help you guys?"

"We nearly hit a panther on the road last night," Ben said. "I ran into a ditch to avoid it."

"Driving after dark can be tough," the ranger said. "Lots of wildlife crossing. So you didn't actually hit the cat?"

Ben shook his head. "No, I'm sure I didn't."

"Good. I would have had to fill out a report. I hate paperwork."

"I think the panther was running from something," Ben said.

Ranger Carl looked doubtful. "Not much scares those cats. They're pretty big."

"I think it was a person," Ben said. "In a thick fur coat."

Ranger Carl laughed. "Then I hope you gave the poor guy a lift to the hospital. He was probably close to heatstroke."

"Probably," Ben said. "Can you think of any reason someone would wander around in the swamps in a fur coat?"

The ranger shrugged. "We had a guy years ago who used to wear a bearskin sometimes. He was crazy." He paused and frowned. "You know, I wouldn't put it past Tanya. She makes a good bit of money off tourists with that Skunk Ape foolishness."

"How does she make money from it?" Gabe asked.

Ranger Carl laughed. "She sells Skunk Ape photos online. And bits of fur and plaster casts of footprints. She had a bone on an auction site once. I'm pretty sure it was from a bear."

Gabe thought about that. It certainly made sense. Ms. Heath was tall, but the creature Gabe saw in the brush looked huge.

"You know," Ben said after they walked away from the ranger, "I think we should drive over to Ms. Heath's Skunk Ape Discovery Center. I wouldn't mind a look around. It would be interesting."

They checked in on Sean and Tyler at the cabin. Sean had cleared up a few frames but they were still confusing. To Gabe, it looked more and more like someone in a furry suit. "I'll keep working on it," Sean said.

Tyler offered to go along to meet with Ms. Heath, so they were soon on their way to the Skunk Ape Discovery Center. It wasn't hard to spot. Homemade signs along the road counted down the miles to the center. The big wooden Skunk Ape photo op sat in front of a battered metal building with a huge painting of a snarling primate on the side.

"Grab the camera and lets get some footage of the front of the building," Ben said. "We'll definitely want to include this place. I can record some voice-over later."

Gabe hopped out of the van with the video camera. He aimed it at the front door when it flew open and Ms. Heath came out. She walked toward the camera, grinning.

"Welcome to the Skunk Ape Discovery Center," she said. "We are the main research center for all Skunk Ape reportings for Florida, Alabama, and Georgia."

"Do you mind if we look inside?" Ben asked.

"Of course not," she said. She practically dragged Ben along with her. For the next hour they looked at Skunk Ape figures, Skunk Ape posters, and Skunk Ape fur swatches. She even had a jar with small brown lumps inside.

Gabe leaned close to the jar. "What's that?"

"Skunk Ape scat," she said. "I collect fur and scat on all my investigations. True researchers are always looking for things like that."

"Scat?" Gabe whispered to his brother.

Ben leaned close to him. "Poop."

Gabe wrinkled his nose.

"Do you have a Skunk Ape costume?" Ben asked.

Ms. Heath frowned. "Why would I want one?"

Ben shrugged. "Seems like Skunk Ape enthusiasts would like one for costume parties."

She looked interested, nodding slowly. "I hadn't thought of that." She seemed fascinated by the idea.

"So you don't already have a costume?"

She shook her head. "But it's a fantastic idea. Do you think it should have some kind of lifts in the shoes? Oh, and maybe glowing eyes. I could use flashlight bulbs." She hurried over to the counter and started taking notes.

Gabe and Ben exchanged looks. It certainly sounded like she hadn't thought about costumes before. "Maybe she's acting?" Gabe whispered.

"I don't think she's that good," Ben whispered back.

They shot a little more footage, then headed

67

back to the cabin to pack for their overnight in the swamp.

"Everyone in the van," Ben called finally.

Gabe looked at his brother in surprise. "I thought we were hiking deeper into the swamp from here."

Ben shook his head. "I have a different spot in mind."

They drove away from the campgrounds, following a winding back road. Finally Ben pulled off. "We'll hike from here," he said. He unfolded a map to go over the route again.

"This is not a good use of my strengths," Sean complained as Tyler and Gabe hiked the pack onto his back.

"Everyone carries," Ben said. His pack was the biggest. Gabe doubted he could even pick it up. Sometimes he forgot what a big guy his brother really was.

They walked deeper into the swamp for

only a short distance, then turned. They walked parallel to the road for a while. Gabe wondered if Ben thought the Skunk Ape really did hang out around the roads.

The heat and humidity felt like breathing soup. Sweat trickled down Gabe's back. It ran down his face and into his eyes. He wiped his face with the hem of his shirt over and over. He wished they were hunting the Yeti instead of the Skunk Ape. It would be cooler in Nepal.

Finally Ben chose a hidden spot in the center of some thick brush. Gabe was shocked by the choice. Ordinarily Ben would avoid a spot like that since all kinds of wildlife liked such hidden places, including things that bite. "You really want us to spend the night here?" he asked.

Bcn nodded. "It's important that we stay hidden and as quiet as possible."

chapter 9

GABE MEETS BIGFOOT

They set up only one tent to help keep the location hidden. "Sleeping is going to be very cozy," Tyler grumbled.

They didn't build a fire, so supper was granola bars and beef jerky. They ate in silence. It was the weirdest camping Gabe had ever done.

The shadowy swamp grew darker. Ben handed out night vision goggles. He rigged a night vision camera on a helmet. He put the helmet on and handed another camera to Gabe.

Ben pulled out a digital recorder and handed it over to Tyler. "I want lots of swamp noise to use as background for some of the other parts of the episode."

"We've got plenty of that here," Tyler whispered back. "Between the rustling, buzzing, and weird honks, it's noisier than the locker room in my gym class."

A snarling shriek cut through the night. Sean smiled. "Now *that's* a Florida panther."

"Swell," Tyler said.

"You guys stay right here. I'm going to go check it out," Ben whispered as he scrambled out of the brush and headed toward the sound.

Gabe sat frozen for a moment, then stood.

"Hey," Tyler said. "Ben told us to wait."

"I've got the second camera," Gabe whispered back. "How can we do the show without a camera shooting Ben? He just told us to stay because he thinks we're kids."

"We are kids," Sean said.

Gabe scrambled out of the hiding place. It was harder than Ben made it look. In the dark, it was really easy to trip over something.

Finally Gabe was on clear ground again and trotting through the swamp in the direction Ben had taken. The ground beneath his feet was like a sponge. He moved as quietly as he could, not wanting Ben to catch him and send him back with the others.

Gabe panned the clearing with his camera, hoping he was still on a straight line toward Ben. The guys would never let him live it down if he got himself lost.

He heard a loud rustling in the brush beyond the clearing. "Ben?" he squeaked.

Something broke through the brush, but it wasn't Ben. A panther ran into the clearing and stopped. The cat curled its upper lip and peered around. Gabe stood perfectly still and tried to look invisible.

It didn't work. The cat's tail lashed and it lowered its head with a rumbling growl. "Nice kitty," Gabe whispered.

The cat growled again and then took a step toward him.

Another rustle in the brush came from behind him. Gabe tried to look in two places at once. He really didn't need another panther.

What stepped from the brush behind him was two-legged. For an instant of wild joy, Gabe thought it was Ben. Then more details kicked in. It was big, far bigger than Ben. It was hairy and it smelled horrible. It had to be a Skunk Ape. Up close, it looked *nothing* like a guy in a suit.

The Skunk Ape stepped around Gabe and hooted softly at the panther. The big cat growled back. The Skunk Ape took another step closer to the cat and hooted again. The cat darted away, crashing back into the brush.

"Oh, wow," Gabe breathcd.

The Skunk Ape turned at the sound. It looked down at Gabe and tilted its head to one side. Then it reached out a huge hand and lightly touched Gabe's night vision goggles. Gabe thought he might pass out.

Loud voices sounded just beyond the clearing and Gabe recognized one of them as Ben. "How could you do something like that?" Ben demanded. The voice that answered back was quieter.

At the sound of the voices, the Skunk Ape hooted again and headed back into the brush behind Gabe. "Wait," Gabe whispered. That's when he remembered that he really should be shooting his encounter. He raised the camera, but all he caught was the furry back as the Skunk Ape headed back into the brush.

He crossed the clearing and headed toward the voices.

Ben yelled as he faced someone nearly as furry as the actual Skunk Ape. He held a Skunk Ape mask in one hand and thc furry front of a Skunk Ape coat in his other fist. "You're supposed to protect the panthers. They're critically endangered."

"They should be extinct," the other man said. Gabe recognized him at once. It was Ranger Carl. "There's no room for them in Florida anymore."

"What makes you hate them so much?" Gabe asked.

"Gabe," Ben snapped. "I told you to stay at the campsite."

While Ben's head was turned, the ranger kicked him hard in the knee and wrenched himself loose. He ran at Gabe, shoved him aside, and disappeared into the brush. Ben limped after him and Gabe followed.

Suddenly they heard a loud growling shriek, then a scream that was definitely human. They broke into the clearing where Gabe had seen the panther and the Skunk Ape. The ranger lay sprawled on the ground.

Ben rushed to the man, checking him for wounds. It wasn't long before the ranger came around. He'd only fainted. He clung to Ben and

76

babbled, "It tried to get me. Don't let it get me."

"Well, you tried to chase it out in front of a car," Ben said as he hauled the trembling man to his feet.

The ranger didn't respond. His eyes darted around at the brush and he kept saying something had tried to get him. Gabe suspected he wasn't talking about the panther.

chapter 10

CAUGHT
ON VIDEO

They didn't end up spending the whole night in the swamp. The ranger practically clung to Ben as they broke camp and headed back to the car. Instead of driving to the campground, they took the ranger to the nearest police station.

Gabe waited until they were finally back to the cabin to tell them about his experience.

"There was another guy in a Skunk Ape suit?" Ben said. "We should have told the police so they could look for him."

Gabe shook his head. "It wasn't a guy in a suit."

"Of course it was. They had some kind of deal with a local orange grower to get rid of the panthers in the area. Ranger Carl said he got paid for every car accident that killed a panther."

"I saw this thing close up," Gabe insisted. "It touched my goggles. It wasn't a guy in a suit. It was a Skunk Ape. I'm pretty sure it's what scared Ranger Carl into fainting."

Tyler flopped into a chair and started pulling off soggy sneakers. "It makes more sense that he just ran into the panther. We know there was one in the area. We heard it. You saw it."

"Yeah, I saw the panther," Gabe said, then he held up the camera. "And I saw the Skunk Ape. I caught it on video."

"Let's plug it in and look," Sean suggested. "Then we'll know."

Of course, what they saw was the shaggy back of the Skunk Ape as it headed into the brush. Still, even Ben had to admit it didn't look like the fur coat the ranger had worn. "He didn't have an outfit anywhere near that good."

"That's because this isn't an outfit," Gabe said, pointing at the screen. "This is a Skunk Ape. It saved me from the panther, and it kept Ranger Carl from getting away."

Ben stared at the screen for a long moment. "Maybe."

When the show about the Skunk Ape finally aired, Ben included an interview with Gabe about what he'd seen that night. They showed the footage from Ben's camera with the ranger in the fake Skunk Ape suit and the footage of Gabe's Skunk Ape slipping into the brush. It was easy to tell the two were very different.

"So did my brother see a real Skunk Ape?" Ben asked in the closing voice-over. "Or was there just another poacher with a better wardrobe? We may never know. You've seen the evidence. You'll have to decide this one for yourself."

Gabe knew that even Tyler and Sean had their doubts, but he didn't. The search for Bigfoot had been a success. He'd seen a real Skunk Ape. He could hardly wait to see what they ran into next!